IT LIVES UNDER MY BED

MONSTER FILES BOOK 1

A. E. STANFILL

1

MOVING IS ROUGH

Bryan being fourteen and being forced to move away from the only friends he had ever known didn't help all the things he was feeling. The only thing that kept his mind off things was the new house. It was a two story what some would call plantation house. He didn't understand what that meant but he was sure it was something cool.

When they settled in Bryan wanted to explore every inch of the home. "Bryan! You need to pick a room and start unpacking!" His mom shouted.

"I know mom!" He shouted back.

"Dinners at six don't be late or the food will get cold!"

"Again, I know!" Bryan wasn't hungry and didn't really care if he ate or not. He spent the last couple of hours trying to pick out a room. And after careful consideration he found the room that suited him most.

To him it was perfect, the color of the room was hunter green. It was very spacious and had two overly large windows. He spent the rest of the night getting his room ready. Putting the bed together and unpacking boxes until his mother made him get ready for bed.

The young man did his normal routine. He took his shower, brushed his teeth, got his clothes ready for the next day. And even though he was angry he still told both his parents and his little sister goodnight.

Bryan then changed into his PJ's and jumped into bed. He tried his best to fall asleep but all he could think of was his friends back home that he had left behind. They were all he had ever known. And now he was forced to start all over.

He understood why they had to move. His dad had been offered a great job just thirty minutes away. And if he was going to better himself and his family he couldn't say no.

It still didn't make it any easier on Bryan and at times he didn't want to accept the fact. Anger had still found its way back to him when he thought of everything he was forced to give up. Though no matter how he felt it doesn't change the outcome.

Bryan had to learn to accept things the way they were and just move on from there. Perhaps this little town wouldn't be so bad if he gives it a chance. Sleep was starting to take over his thoughts and his mind began to calm.

As the night went on and midnight approached. Something strange began to happen. Bryan woke up to the sound of voices filling his room. They were very faint but he could tell someone or something was in his room.

"Who's there?" Bryan nervously whispered. The whispers had stopped and he chalked it up to nerves. When he tried to fall back to sleep the whispers started again. Yet this time it felt like his bed was being moved or shaken.

Bryan jumped out of bed wide awake. This time he was for sure it wasn't a bad dream or nerves. He rushed over and flipped the light switch. Bryan searched high and low thinking his sister was maybe hiding in his room.

There was still one place in the room that he had yet to search and that was underneath his bed. He was a little scared but managed to suck it up and inch closer towards the bed. Then he suddenly stopped in his tracks after the bed shook slightly.

Bryan cleared his throat, "Who's there?" he asked again. "If that's you Matty it's not funny." He stayed about a foot away and found the courage to kneel down. He took a quick glance under the bed but nothing was there.

He stood back up and scratched his head out of confusion. What in the world was going on, he just couldn't figure it out. Perhaps he would just go back to bed and tell his parents what had happened in the morning.

The rest of the night went by fairly quiet, the only thing he heard was his dad snoring. And his bed didn't move again which allowed the young man to fall asleep for the second time.

Morning came quicker than he hoped it would. Rays of light shined through his window beating down on his face waking him up. Bryan pulled the covers over his head refusing to get out of bed.

Moments later he could hear his mom marching up the steps muttering words of disapproval under her breath. She stopped at his door and started knocking loud and hard.

"Get out of bed this instance, Bryan Sanders," she said angrily. "Breakfast is downstairs and you know the rules of the house. We eat together as a family before everyone's day starts."

"Yes, mother," he replied. His mom went back downstairs the same way she came up angry at him. Bryan raised up and stretched his arms into the air letting out a long yawn before getting out of bed.

He threw on his clothes that he had picked out for the day. Brushed his teeth then went running downstairs to join his family at the table. "Look who finally decided to join us," his dad grunted.

"Sorry, dad," Bryan responded.

"You don't look so good either. Long night?"

The young man put his face in his hands, "A very long night," he mumbled.

"Look I get it," his dad said. "New home, a different environment. It hasn't been easy on any of us."

He looked over at his dad through his fingers, "It's not that," he grumbled.

His mom insisted he put his hands down and have a conversation like a normal person. As she was placing the meal on the table. When they were half way through breakfast his mom decided to break the silence. "Well?"

"Well what?" He asked.

"Are you going to tell us about last night?" She asked. It was clear she wasn't going to let this go the look on her face gave that away.

"Not with Matty at the table."

"Why not?" His father questioned.

"I don't want to scare her."

After breakfast was over and his little sister went off to play. Bryan explained the odd events that plagued him last night. Both his mom and dad sat there trying to keep a straight face. To him this was no joking matter and was starting to get upset.

"Why are you trying not to laugh?" Bryan grunted. "This isn't funny." His mom began clearing off the table and his dad grabbed the morning paper without saying a word. "Am I being ignored now?"

"Nope," his dad responded with his face hidden on the other side of the newspaper.

"Why don't you go play outside, make some new friends!" She shouted from the kitchen.

"You heard your mom," his dad said. "Go play outside."

Bryan stood from the table, turned and stomped out the front door. He was upset and a little hurt that his parents didn't listen to him yet again.

2

MAKING NEW FRIENDS

THE YOUNG MAN WALKED THE STREETS OF THE small town of Manila. There wasn't really much to the town. He managed to find a couple small grocery stores. A candy store combined with a small arcade with pool tables.

It looked like the arcade was packed full of kids about his age and older. Though at that moment he didn't feel like it was the right time to walk in there as the new kid. And on top of that he didn't have any money to spend.

So he walked on past the arcade and towards the park area. The park seemed like a very cool place to hang out. There were two basketball courts, a tennis court, two baseball fields. And to top it off there was a large swimming pool smack in the middle of it all.

With how hot it was outside he would have loved to go swimming. Unfortunately it was closed this summer due to repairs. Just his luck, his first year dealing with hundred degree temps and the best place to cool off was closed down.

"Hey, do you play basketball?" A voice called out. Bryan turned to see three young teen boys standing there looking at him. "Well?"

Bryan shrugged, "Yeah I play," he replied.

"Great, we need a fourth player," the boy smiled. "I'm Brandon by the way." He pointed over towards the skinny blond headed kid, "That's Jason." Then over towards the heavy set kid who seemed to have a bit of an attitude, "Last but not least is Jimmy."

"Nice to meet you guys my name is Bryan."

Jimmy threw the basketball at him, "Doesn't matter what your name is as long as you can play."

Bryan proved to be better than all three of them. And when the first game was over the three teens argued over who would be on his team next. The young men played basketball for hours on end. It looked as though Bryan had made his first friends and that felt great.

When they were done playing the four young men took a seat on a picnic table. Bryan asked them questions about their town. And they asked him questions about where he moved from and what it was like there.

"What house did you move into?" Brandon questioned.

"A very old two story house. I believe it was called the Hillside Estate," Bryan answered. The three teens looked at one another. Their eyes wide and their facial expressions changed as well. "Is something wrong?" He asked.

"You live there?" Jason gasped.

Bryan looked confused, "Yeah. Why?" he asked.

"That place is haunted," Jimmy belted out.

Bryan chuckled, "You guys are pulling my leg," he replied.

Brandon looked the most serious of the three, "They're not joking," he said. "Everyone in town knows that house is haunted."

"What proof do you have?"

Jason sighed, "With all the stories we've heard and the way the adults don't want to talk about the place. What more proof do we need?"

"I want to hear these stories," Bryan smirked.

All three boys told Bryan of the stories they have heard about the old house. About how other families moved out quickly because of what the house did to their kids. And all the stories revolved around the kids talking about something underneath their beds.

They talked about hearing voices and their beds being moved or bumped. And that was just the start of things. From what they heard it only got worse. Some of the kids claimed that their bed would fly across the room. While others said they had been pulled underneath.

Nobody really knows what it is. Some said it was a monster while others claimed it was a ghost. But it all ends the same, the kids were so scared the parents would eventually move out. Leave town never to be heard from again, they just leave.

Bryan cleared his throat trying his best to act tough, "That's the craziest thing I've ever heard," he said. Trying not to show the fact that he was scared.

Jason jumped up like a bolt of lightning had hit him, "I have to get home!" He exclaimed. "My parents are going to kill me!" And off he went running down the sidewalk with Jimmy right behind him.

Brandon shook his head and laughed, "Guess I should get home too," he said. "Oh before I forget. If you ever do have anything weird happen. Give Miller and Smith a call, look them up in the phone book. I think they call themselves The Monster Files or something like that. See you around Bryan." And off he went.

That night after dinner and movie night with his family it was time for Bryan to get ready for bed. This made him nervous and somewhat scared of what the night would bring. He tried his best to avoid going to his room.

When his mom caught onto this she forced him to go upstairs and get ready for bed. And not to argue because that wasn't the type of kid he was. Bryan went on to do his nightly routine then went to his room. He stared at his bed for a few minutes waiting for it to move.

Nothing happened, no movement, no voices, no nothing. Maybe his dad was right, last night could have just been first night jitters. He flipped the switch and the light went off. Bryan jumped into bed, pulled the covers over his head and closed his eyes.

When the clock struck midnight the voices came back. Very quietly at first then louder, loud enough to wake Bryan up. He jumped up and looked around the room. Again it started at the sametime it did the night before.

Again the bed started to move ever so slightly. And like the story he heard his bed slid across the room with him in it. He leaped out of bed dropping his late night snack on the floor. Bryan ran over and flipped the light back on.

He was scared now more than ever before. To have his bed move that far across the room on its own has never happened to him before. Bryan took a deep breath and nervously approached the bed.

What caught the young man by surprise was when a hand reached out from under the bed and grabbed his candy bar. Bryan went running out of his room shouting at the top of his lungs. Waking everyone in the house up and that didn't set well with his parents.

Bryan tried to explain the situation to his parents. He even begged them to take a look in his room at his bed. He swore up and down that something was under his bed and moved it across the room.

He opened his door and pleaded that his parents walk inside. When they did his parents were even more upset. Nothing had been moved, not a damn thing. The bed was in the same spot it had always been. Nothing in his room had changed at all.

When they insisted it was just a nightmare Bryan threw a fit. He was upset when they refused to listen to him. It was like when they first told him they were moving. He didn't want to move and leave his friends behind but did they listen? No. Just like now. Are they listening? No.

The young man stomped back inside his room and

slammed the door behind him. He could hear his parents voicing their displeasure with him as they made their way back to their own room.

Bryan walked over to the bed and grabbed the covers. He curled up in a corner covering himself up. For the first time he felt alone, parents that refuse to listen to him and no friends to talk with. He was going to have to handle this one on his own but not alone.

3

MEET THE MONSTER FILES

THE MORNING CAME SLOWLY BUT SURELY. BRYAN had never been so happy to see the sunrise. It meant that he was safe for another day. He was tired but that wasn't going to stop him from doing what needed to be done.

He jumped to his feet, got dressed and ran out the door not even looking back. Not that he exactly wanted to look back at that dreadful bed. "You're up early," his mom said when he ran down the stairs.

Bryan grabbed the phone book and took a seat at the table. "I have something I need to do," he replied, flipping through the pages of the phone book.

"Do tell," she smiled.

Bryan didn't exactly want to explain to his mom what he was up to. He knew that she would disapprove of his actions. "I made a couple of friends and I wanted to find their phone numbers," he responded.

"Okay, if you find their numbers you can call them after breakfast," she told him.

Bryan scarfed his breakfast down and picked up the phone book after excusing himself from the table. He sat down on the couch in the living room flipping through the pages. The number he was looking for was found in the very back of the phone book.

"I found their number," Bryan announced. "Can I give them a call mom?"

"I already said that you could," she replied. "Just don't take too long, I'm expecting a call soon."

"You should have bought me a cellphone,"

Bryan smuggly replied.

"Never going to happen," his mom told him.

Bryan rolled his eyes before picking up the phone. He dialed the number, it rang a few times before someone finally answered. "Monster Files," a young males voice answered. "This is Miller. What can I do for you?"

"Um....My name is Bryan," he responded hesitantly.

"You don't have to be nervous," Miller laughed. "Tell me Bryan. Why have given us a call?"

"I may be in need of some help," Bryan replied.

"Help with what?" Miller questioned.

"Well it all started when we first moved here a few days ago." Bryan replied. "The first night I heard voices coming from under my bed. After that my bed started to move slightly. I brushed it off as a dream.

And it only got worse from there. My bed now moves across the floor and I've even seen a hand reach out and grab my snacks and pull them under the bed. I know it sounds crazy but I'm telling the truth."

"What do your parents think?" Miller asked.

"They refused to listen to me," said Bryan.

"Most parents don't want to believe us," Miller responded. "Anyways. Where do you live?"

"Hillside Estate," Bryan answered.

"Hmm....I've heard of that place," Miller replied.

"I was told it was haunted," Bryan said.

"We need to talk face to face," said Miller. "Do you know where the little ice cream shop is at?"

"I do," Bryan replied.

"Good," he said. "Meet me there tomorrow after lunch."

That night Bryan decided he didn't want to sleep in his bed. Instead he made a fort out of his blankets and slept in there for the night. It was the first night of good sleep he had gotten in a while. To make things even stranger nothing happened. No voices, his bed didn't move, if anything it was a normal night.

After Bryan's family time at the table. He hugged his mom and dad and apologized for his actions as of late. If he was going to get any further with this situation he needed to earn back his parents trust.

Later on after lunch the young man made his way towards town. Meeting up with Miller at the ice cream shop. Except Miller wasn't alone there was a young girl sitting across the table from him. And she's the one that looked up at him standing there. She then looked at Miller and whispered something to him.

Miller turned and greeted Bryan waving him over to

the table. Bryan went over and took a seat at the table. "Want some ice cream?" Miller politely asked.

Bryan shook his head, "No thank you," he responded. Miller with his thick Clark Kent glasses along with wearing a suit. Made the kid look like a bit of a nerd.

Miller felt a foot kick the side of his leg, "Where are my manners," he laughed. "This is my friend and partner in crime Smith." His friend or partner looked more like a normal teen. She had her long blonde reddish hair pulled back into a ponytail. And to Bryan she was really cute, he even felt himself blush a little.

"It's Diane Smith," she belted out. "Franky loves to keep calling us by last names only."

"My name is Frank! FRANK! Not Franky!" he angrily said. "I hate it when you call me that."

"Gets him every time," she smirked.

"Can we get down to business please," Miller grumbled.

"Take all the fun out of it," Smith sighed. She turned to face Bryan, "So my partner here told me you're having problems at home."

Bryan was quick to correct her, "I'm having problems with whatever is under my bed," he said.

"Do you really think something is living under your bed?" Smith questioned.

"It's either that or a ghost," Bryan replied. "I did hear the house was haunted."

Miller was quick to point out that it wasn't a ghost. Seeing how a hand reached out from under the bed to grab a candybar. He also explained how he felt the whole town was strange. Weird things happen in this little town all the time.

That's why Smith and himself started Monster Files. Because the strange things only happen to the kids for some reason. And they want to help where the adults want to ignore the situation. Bryan was caught by surprise learning the story of the town. But still just wanted to know what was under his bed.

"So then what's under my bed?" Bryan asked.

"Not sure," Miller responded. "I do believe that whatever it is only shows up when there are kids living in the house. Nothing happens when it's just grownups living there."

"Then what do I do?" Bryan grunted. "I can't even sleep in my own bed. There has to be something you can do."

"Give us a couple of days," Miller insisted. "We'll figure it out."

"Or it could be in your head," Smith responded.

"It's not in my head," Bryan hissed.

"We'll see," she smiled.

4

FINDING AN ANSWER

OVER THE NEXT COUPLE OF DAYS MILLER WORKED very hard to figure out what could be under Bryan's bed. While Smith was trying to prove that this was all in Bryan's head. What they considered their base of operations. Was a treehouse that Miller's Dad built for him a few years ago.

Miller had pictures and reports of all the different mysteries and monsters that had been reported in the small town. He believed some were of kids' imaginations and some to be true. While Smith didn't believe in the supernatural her way of thinking was that there was a simple answer for everything.

Miller went through everything and came up with nothing. Which was getting closer to proving Smith right. And he hated that more than anything. Deep down Miller knew Bryan was telling the truth. And he was going to help him out any way he could.

"Come up with anything yet?" Smith asked with a smug look on her face.

"Not yet," Miller grumbled. "But I'm not giving up."

"What else can you do?" She questioned.

"I plan on staying the night at his house," he answered. "That way I can find the answer I'm looking for."

"And if you don't find anything?" She replied.

"Then I will admit you're right about this one," he responded.

"An easy win for me," Smith smiled.

"Hey, this isn't over yet," said Miller.

Later in the day Miller called the number that Bryan had given to him. Bryan's Mom was the one that answered the phone. She sounded like a nice lady. Miller asked if he could speak with Bryan.

Moments later Bryan answered the phone, "Hello," he said.

"It's me, Miller."

Bryan couldn't have been happier to hear his voice. "Please tell me you found something," he happily said.

"Sorry, we haven't found anything yet," Miller responded. "But I have an idea that could help."

"What's your idea?" Bryan asked.

"Ask your Mom if you can have a friend spend the night," Miller responded. "If she says it's okay, I will bring what we need over with me tonight."

"Let me see what she says," Bryan replied with a slight sigh. Miller could hear muffled voices, guess Bryan didn't want him to hear what they were talking about. "She said it was okay. I have to do my chores, so come over around five."

"Great," Miller responded. "I will tell my parents and see you tonight." Miller turned and grinned at Smith, "Tonight I will show you proof that monsters exist."

"Yeah, yeah," she huffed. "Don't get your hopes up."

Miller gathered his things from the treehouse that he would need. Including the most important thing of all, his video camera. He was going to prove to Smith that this was real with actual video footage.

Then he ran inside his house to let his parents know that he was staying with a friend. But he wasn't going to leave the house without doing his fair share of work. He, like Bryan, was forced to finish his chores before he could go anywhere.

Once he was done he gathered a few candy bars he had stashed away for late night snacks. Miller put everything in a small duffle bag along with a change of clothes and pj's. He told his Mom and Dad that he loved them. Thanked them for letting him stay at a friend's house and ran out the door.

Miller didn't need or want a ride from his parents. It was such a small town you could get from point A to B within a mile walk. And if he witnessed anything strange he could record it for his files.

To his dismay his walk to Bryan's house proved uneventful. He stood outside of the estate looking over the house. It was creepy that much was for sure. The house was old and could very well be haunted. But something in the pit of Miller's stomach told him otherwise.

Frank walked up to the door and knocked a couple of times. Bryan's Mom opened the door and greeted him with a smile. She warmly welcomed him into her home. Then she called Bryan downstairs. The young man came running down the stairs like he was shot out of a cannon.

"What have I told you about running in this house young man?" his mother scolded.

"Not to do it," Bryan grumbled.

"Things would be a lot easier on us both if you would just listen."

"Yes Mom," said Bryan. "I'm sorry. Can we go now?"

His Mom rolled her eyes and huffed, "Go, but be back down for dinner," he said.

"Come on." Bryan looked at Miller, "My room is up there."

The young man led Miller up the stairs and to the left. Bryan opened the bedroom door, "Here it is," he said. "My room. And there's my bed, the scariest thing in this whole house."

"Do these strange events happen all the time?" Miller questioned.

"Nope," Bryan answered. "Seems to only happen at midnight."

"Hmm...It's going to be a long night," Miller jokingly replied.

"What should we do in the meantime?"

"Set everything up and then we wait," Miller responded. "Good thing I brought plenty of snacks."

"We just wait?" Bryan responded.

"Nothing else we can do," Miller shrugged. "I will start setting up my video camera."

It took no longer than thirty minutes to set up his video camera at the angle he preferred. It gave them the rest of the time to get to know each other better. Miller explained more about Monster Files and Smith and himself.

While Bryan talked about himself and where he was from. He spoke of his friends back home and how he missed them. He also spoke of his parents and his little sister. Even though he was upset they were still his family and he loved them.

"Bryan!" His Mom shouted. "It's dinner time!"

"Come on," Bryan said. "You know how parents are if you keep them waiting."

The two boys made their way downstairs and took a set at the table with Bryan's parents and sister. Both Bryan and Miller ate like most young teens do. Scarfing down the food in front of them like they were both starving.

When dinner was over and Bryan's family was done being nosey. They were told they could stay for movie night or head back upstairs. Miller was curious but that choice was Bryan's to make because he was there to do a job.

Bryan decided what the heck. Might as well watch a movie and eat some popcorn while they waited. It was one of those cheesy black and white movies that his Dad loved so much. Curse of Dracula was what it was called.

Bryan was bored but always enjoyed the family time and popcorn. Miller seemed to be into the movie though it was his cup of tea. When the movie was over Bryan told his parents and sister goodnight.

They headed up the steps and Miller went and placed candy bars around the bed. "Does anything happen when you're awake?" he asked Bryan.

"Not sure," Bryan answered. "My Mom never lets me stay up late."

"What time do you usually go to bed?" Was the next question.

"Around ten."

"Has anything happened since you've been sleeping on the floor?" Miller questioned.

Bryan had a surprised look on his face, "How do you know I sleep on the floor?" He asked.

"It's clear you haven't slept in your bed," Miller replied. "So has anything happened lately?"

"Strangely. No," Bryan answered.

"Then it's settled," Miller replied.

"What is settled?" Bryan grunted.

"We both have to sleep in the bed," Miller said.

"I don't think so," Bryan grumbled. "Nobody sleeps in my bed but me."

"We don't have a choice here," Miller insisted.

"No," Bryan hissed.

Miller shrugged, "Okay, looks like you will have to deal with whatever is under your bed. At least until your parents decide to move," he replied.

"Fine," Bryan sighed. "Guess I have no choice."

"Look," Miller chuckled. "All we have to do is lay in bed quietly until something happens."

When Bryan and Miller were laying in the bed. Bryan quietly asked why Miller had placed Candy bars around the bed. Miller explained that it was to lure whatever was under the bed out in the open. And the video camera would capture it as proof for Smith.

Later that night the two young men had accidentally fallen asleep. That is until the clock struck midnight. Just like all the other times the voices had returned. Which woke both the young men up. Bryan wanted to jump out of the bed but Miller stopped him.

Miller put his finger to his lips. Signaling for Bryan to keep quiet. The voices became louder before the bed slightly moved. Almost as if the bed had been bumped by accident. Moments later the bed slowly moved across the floor. Then it moved right back to where the bed stood in the first place.

The bed started to violently tremble, like whatever it was wanted them off the mattress. Bryan tried again to jump off the bed but Miller was having none of it. "When I let you go run for the door but do not leave the room," Miller whispered.

Bryan did as Miller had said he jumped out of bed and ran for the door then stopped. He looked back at the bed as Miller peaked over the edge. Fear swelled up inside Bryan when he noticed the yellow eyes staring back at him from under the bed.

Bryan stood there and watched in horror as a hand for the second time grabbed all the candy bars. That was the last thing he remembered before everything went dark. When he awoke Miller was standing over him. It must have been as rays of warm light were shining in his eyes.

5

NAME THAT MONSTER

"What happened?" Bryan asked, as he tried to clear the cobwebs in his head.

"You blacked out," Miller responded. "Must have seen something really scary to cause that."

"It was scary," Bryan replied. "I've never seen eyes like that before."

"Eye's?" Miller said with a hint of surprise. "The only thing I saw was a hand grab the candy."

"What about the camera? Did you not watch what was recorded?" Bryan questioned.

Miller helped Bryan to his feet, "We need a VCR for that," he said. "Tell me more about the eyes."

"Yellow," he said.

"What?" Miller responded.

"It had yellow eyes," Bryan gasped. "Yellow glowing eyes. I've seen the hand before but the yellow eyes were the first."

"That gives me something to work with at least," said Miller.

"So what now?" Bryan questioned.

"I have to get back and talk with Smith and watch the recording," Miller insisted.

"Please let me know what you find out," Bryan said almost pleadingly.

"I will," Miller replied. "But for now keep sleeping on the floor."

"You don't have to tell me twice," Bryan jokingly said.

"Oh and one more thing."

"What?"

"Leave candy around the bed at night," Miller answered.

"Why?" Bryan's brow raised.

"Just a hunch for now," Miller replied.

Miller gave Bryan a knuckle bump and assured him that he would have an answer before too long. Miller skipped having breakfast with the Sanders. But he did thank them for letting him stay the night. He wished them well, told them to have a good day before heading out the door.

Later that day he met Smith at the treehouse. She was quick to question him about how the night went. Miller explained every little detail from the other night. Smith was reluctant and had her doubts. But some of those doubts, not all, were put to rest when they watched the video.

It showed the glowing yellow eyes that Bryan spoke of. And when the hand reached out from under the bed

Smith was quick to press the pause button. She sat close to the screen and studied the hand.

Miller was curious so he questioned what she was looking at with such focus. She explained that the hand looked old. More human than monster. The hand also hand fingernails instead of claws. Of course they were curved under and perhaps very sharp.

Smith also pointed out the wrinkles of the skin. The scars on the back of the hand and the warts on top of those. Miller was getting anxious and wanted Smith to get to the point. If she had any ideas on what they were dealing with then he had to know as well.

"I think it's a witch," Smith muttered.

Miller leaned his head in closer, "It's a what?" he asked.

"A witch," she said out loud.

Miller smiled brightly, "I thought you didn't believe in monsters," he replied.

"Witches are not monsters," she grumbled.

"Then what are they?" he asked.

"Humans that study witchcraft," she responded.

"Humans that found a way to live forever?" he questioned with glee.

Smith shrugged, "Maybe," she said.

"Whatever Diane," he snorted. "What kind of witch are we dealing with?"

She had to think about it for a moment. "More than likely a folklore witch," Smith answered.

"What is that?" Miller asked.

"A witch that has managed to stay alive for many many years," she answered.

"How?" he asked.

"I don't know," Smith replied. "Never thought I would ever find one."

"How do we stop it?" he questioned.

"How am I supposed to know," Smith hissed. "But I know how we might find out."

"The Library," Miller said with excitement.

"Exactly," Smith agreed.

Miller and Smith hopped on their bicycles and headed for the library. It wasn't that far and they managed to make it there in a matter of minutes. The librarian told them both right off the bat to keep it down. Because the last time they were here it got loud very loud. And it had annoyed the librarian enough she had kicked them out.

Both apologised more times than once. And again just before walking further inside. Smith went her way and Miller went his. Both on a mission to find out what kind of witch could possibly be bothering Bryan at night. And what it might want and try and do next.

Miller was going through different types of folklore books and old nursery rhymes. Some mentioned witches but not the kind of witch he was searching for.

Smith was sitting across the table from him going through her pile of books. Unlike Miller she however did find something of interest. It was about a certain type of witch. It spoke of witches terrorising families' kids. The older brother or sister more than anyone else.

These witches would come out only at certain times of the night. Midnight to be exact from under the older siblings beds. These witches do not show their faces. Only their yellow eyes and hands that reach out and take things mainly food.

It also says that they scare the older siblings so bad they lose track of everything else. Which leaves the younger sibling unprotected. Then they use the snacks to gain the trust of the younger child. But they have to become friends with the younger child before they can steal their lives away.

They need to do this after so many years or they will indeed die. It's the only way these witches can live forever. Diane coughed slightly to get Miller's attention. He glanced up at her and she pushed the book she was reading over to him.

Miller looked over the book and found the answers he was looking for. But it wasn't going to be the answers Bryan will want to hear. Especially when he learns that his sister is in trouble. Miller looked over the book further but couldn't find anything about stopping the witch.

Then it hit him like a ton of bricks. Miller realised he made a huge mistake. He told Bryan to leave the candy out and around his bed. This was only helping the witch get to his kid sister. Smith could tell by the look on Miller's face that something was wrong.

"What's going on with you Frank?" She asked.

Miller held up his hand signaling for her to just wait. He took out his cellphone and punched in Bryan's home phone number. When Mrs. Sanders answered the phone. Miller did all he could to keep his feelings under control.

"Is Bryan home?" He asked.

The phone went silent for a couple of seconds, "Bryan here. What do you want?" He answered.

"It's me Miller," Frank whispered.

"Why are you whispering?" Bryan asked.

"I'm at the library," he replied. "Just listen to me. Do not sleep in your room tonight. And whatever you do take the snacks out of your room."

"Why?" Bryan questioned.

"I'm not done talking yet. Just listen to me, please. Whatever you do tonight do not leave your sister alone. Make up anything you can just don't leave her alone," Miller explained.

"What is going on?" Bryan asked, with a hint of fear in his voice.

"Just do it!" Miller shouted which got the attention of the librarian. He lowered his head and whispered. "Trust me okay? I need some more time to explain things. I will be at your house bright and early tomorrow," he said before hanging up.

Bryan was wondering what that phone call was all about. But he trusted Miller and did what was asked of him. He didn't let Matty leave his sight. And even talked her into having a brother sister night.

His Mom and Dad didn't complain, they always told him he needed to spend more time with his sister. It was late and Matty was still awake while he was getting tired.

So he decided to bribe her. If she would lay down and be quiet he would read her a bedtime story.

And he did as promised and read her a bedtime story from beginning to end until she fell asleep. Bryan sat on the edge of the bed trying not to fall asleep. All while thinking about that crazy phone call from Miller.

Sleep was starting to take over and his eyes started to close. When he was right at the edge of slumber. He was woken up by something grabbing his shoulder pulling him backwards.

6

THE WITCH COMES OUT OF HIDING

"Scared you," his sister laughed as she was jumping up and down on the bed.

Bryan shook his head and smirked, "We had a deal Matty," he said. "Time to lay down and go to bed."

"I can't," she replied.

"Why not?" Bryan asked.

"Because silly," Matty giggled. "I haven't talked to my friend yet."

"Your friend?" Bryan looked at her confused. "What friend?"

"My friend that lives under my bed," she replied.

Bryan could feel the color fade from his face. Most of the time he would brush that off as his sister's imagination. But when she said friend from under the bed. He knew all too well it was the same thing that stayed under his bed. Now things have become even more serious than before.

Miller showed up at the house the next morning like

he said he would. He was quick about running up to the door and knocked. And this time Bryan was the one that answered the door and he didn't look happy.

He wanted to know what was going on. Smith walked up to the door as well. Both asked if they could come in. Bryan said there were no girls allowed in the house rule when his parents were gone. But he did say they could set out on the porch and talk if that was alright with them.

This time Miller let Smith do all the talking. Seeing how she knew more about witches than he did. And Smith explained it all so that he could understand what was at stake. It was something that Bryan was stunned to hear. Yet now he was scared for her now instead of himself.

"How do we stop it?" Bryan questioned.

"We don't know yet," Miller interrupted.

"But we are going to find out," Smith added.

"Yet she has already made friends with the witch," Bryan responded. "It's only a matter of time before she comes for her."

"We're not going to let that happen," Miller responded.

"How can you stop it?" Bryan asked.

"I will stay the night and we can fight it off together," Miller suggested.

"How can I trust you? You're the one that had the hunch of leaving out more candy. That could have cost my sister her life last night," Bryan replied out of anger.

"Then let me make it up to you by helping you keep your little sister safe tonight," Miller pleaded.

"Fine," Bryan responded with a hint of anger.

"While you guys are doing that I will go back to the library and see what else I can find," Smith said. "Maybe if I'm lucky I can find a way to stop the witch for good."

"Good luck," Miller told her.

"Keep that little girl safe," said Smith.

"I will," he responded.

After Smith rode away on her bicycle Bryan asked Miller if he played football. It caught him off guard but perhaps Bryan just wanted to take his mind off things. Miller wasn't much on sports but if it helped. He would throw the old pigskin around for a bit.

Bryan went inside the house and came back out with the football in hand. He motioned for Miller to follow him around back. Bryan threw the ball through the air towards Miller. He completely missed it of course. Throwing the ball back also proved Miller wasn't much of an athlete.

"Sports isn't your thing is it?" Bryan said as he threw the football towards Miller.

He caught the ball this time, but just barely, "Not really," he replied, throwing the football back.

"What do you do for fun?" Bryan asked.

"I read books about this town's history in my free time," Miller answered.

"That's how you learned so much about Manila," Bryan chuckled.

"Pretty much," Miller laughed.

The two young men stayed outside throwing the football around until almost sunset. Like always Mr.s Sanders opened the front door. And yelled for Bryan letting him know it was time to come inside and clean up for dinner.

Both young men rushed past Mrs. Sanders and into the house. "Bryan. Are you forgetting something?" she questioned.

"Oh yeah." Bryan looked at her bright eyed, "Can my friend stay the night again?" He asked.

"Of course," she answered with a warm smile. "But this is the last time for a while, because your Dad is going out of town on business."

"Yes Mom," Bryan replied.

That night after dinner Bryan asked Matty if him and his new friend could play board games with her. Of course she said yes. What little sister wouldn't want to hangout with their older brother or sister.

Bryan and Miller kept Matty busy for most of the night and away from her bed. When she started to fall asleep. Bryan built her a fort to sleep in. Told her they were protecting the Princess from the Dragons. Her imagination would do the rest for them.

After Matty fell asleep Bryan and Miller stayed awake quietly watching her bed. Miller looked at his watch, it was one minute until midnight. He looked over at Bryan, "Get ready," he whispered. "It's almost time."

What happened next was far different then what they experienced last time. There were no voices, the bed didn't even move, not an inch. Instead the light in the room started to flicker and went out. It was pitch black in the room, good thing Miller brought a couple of flashlights.

He handed one to Bryan and insisted he turn it on. Both flashlights being on brightened up the room just fine. Both young men took a deep breath of relief. That is until Miller watched a hand come out from under the bed. Miller nudged Bryan and looked over at the bed.

Bryan gasped when he watched two hands coming out from under the bed. But that wasn't all, it looked like the witch was about to show herself to them. And she did, the witch's whole body crawled out from under the bed. The witch stood up and was much taller than what the boys expected.

The witch's gray thinning hair covered most of her face. But they could still see her glowing yellow eyes. Her nose was long and curved with a wart on the end. Her teeth were crooked and of a greenish color. She stood hunched over glaring at the teens.

7

A FITTING END

"Where is the child?" The witch hissed.

"You can't have her," Bryan spat.

"I need the child," it hissed again.

"You heard my friend. You can't have her," Miller said without hesitation.

"Give me the child," The witch demanded.

"Screw this." Bryan went to hit the witch with the flashlight. But instead he was sent flying across the room and hit the wall hard. "That was stupid," Bryan grunted in pain.

Miller tried to force the witch back under the bed but that didn't work either. And he found himself getting smacked around the room as well. "How do we stop her?" He thought to himself.

"Enough playing," the witch grumbled. "Give me the girl, I'm hungry."

Bryan got to his feet and put himself in front of the fort. "Not a chance," he replied. Miller got to his feet and stood beside Bryan. It might be stupid to fight a witch but he wasn't going to give up either.

The witch let out a strange sounding giggle. "Foolish boys," she said. "I have fought many like you. They have all failed just like you will. And I will keep on living for a hundred more years."

Miller's cell phone started to ring. It was Smith. "Now's not a good time," he said, breathing heavily.

"The witch has shown herself. Hasn't she?" Smith quickly asked.

"You could say that," Miller responded. "Please tell me you have something. Because right now this thing is beating the shit out of us."

"You can't fight a witch head on," Smith smuggly replied.

"Just tell me how to stop it!" Miller shouted.

"You don't have to yell," Smith responded.

"Smith!" Miller shouted again.

"Okay, okay. Geeze," she muttered. "You have to break the connection with Bryan's sister. She has to see for herself and realize the witch is not her friend. It's the only way to stop it from taking her."

The witch was on top of Bryan before he could stand back up. Miller watched and tried to help but was swatted away like a bug and his glasses went flying off his face. A blue light appeared in front of the witch's mouth. Luckily for Bryan his little sister stepped out of the fort.

"Leave my brother alone!" She shouted.

"We were just playing child no need to be scared," she said, walking away from Bryan and towards Matty.

"Really?" She let out a sigh of relief.

"She's lying to you Matty," Bryan coughed. "She wants to take you away from us. From your family, from me your brother."

"Shut up you wretched brat!" The witch hissed.

Bryan felt as though he had no choice but to call out for his parents' help. "Mom! Dad!" He shouted to the top of his lungs.

The old hag looked back at Bryan, "Your parents can't save her," she keckled. "Neither can you."

One of the flashlights rolled over and bumped Matty's foot. She reached down and picked it up. Then she shined the light towards the witches face. The little girl might have been ten years old but she wasn't stupid. Even she could see that something wasn't right.

"You're not her," Matty gasped. It was like a spell had been broken. She could see its real face. And it wasn't the friendly young face that she remembered from nights before. This was the face of a monster. Not a young princess wanting to take Matty to visit her kingdom.

"It's time to go see my kingdom," the witch told her. "I thought you wanted to go there with me."

"No!" Matty shouted. "You're not a princess! You're an ugly, ugly monster that is trying to hurt my brother."

"But we're friends," the witch insisted.

"We're not friends," Matty yelled. "Go away!"

The witch opened a bag she was carrying and dumped a pile of candy bars on the floor. "Come with me and this candy will be yours." The old hag did her best to try and bribe Matty to come with.

"Go away!" Matty yelled out again. "You tried to hurt my brother! We are not friends! Go away! Go away! Go away!" Matty threw the flashlight hitting the witch in the face.

That angered the old hag and she wanted revenge. But it was too late, she only had a certain amount of time to take Matty away. The clock struck two in the morning. Her time was now up. The old witch let out a scream that echoed throughout the house. Light filled the room and then "boom" the witch exploded.

Glitter filled the room floating down and around the children before the bedroom light flickered back on. It was over, it was finally over. The young children had defeated the witch sending back where she had come from.

Matty was jumping up and down playing in the glitter like it had been one big game. While Bryan and Miller gave each other a fist bump and took a sigh of relief. It wasn't much longer Mr's. Sanders came into the room.

"What is going on here?" She questioned. "And why are you and Matty up past your bedtime?"

"Matty was having nightmares," Bryan answered. "We came in here to keep her company until she falls back asleep."

Mr's. Sanders couldn't get upset about that. Her son and his friend were just being nice which was a good thing. Before she went back to her room she told them to clean up the glitter. Everything was okay now and should be back tomorrow.

Bryan and Miller cleaned up the glitter and let Matty crawl into bed and get some sleep. The two boys went back to Bryans room and got some well needed sleep themselves.

Three days later while Miller and Smith were going over the case they had solved. Bryan showed up at the treehouse. He thanked them both for what they had done for him and Matty. If not for them his sister would have been another kid to have gone missing in that house.

Bryan was also happy to tell them that his family decided to move back home. Both Miller and Smith were happy to hear the great news. They told him to be safe and if he ever needed them just give the Monster Files a call.

Two months later another family moved into the estate. That night when the older sister went to grab a snack off her bed it was gone.

THE
END

Dear reader,

We hope you enjoyed reading *It Lives Under My Bed*. Please take a moment to leave a review, even if it's a short one. Your opinion is important to us.

Discover more books by A.E. Stanfill at
https://www.nextchapter.pub/authors/ae-stanfill

Want to know when one of our books is free or discounted? Join the newsletter at
http://eepurl.com/bqqB3H

Best regards,
A.E. Stanfill and the Next Chapter Team

ABOUT THE AUTHOR

My name is Allen Stanfill, I live in Powell Wyoming with my wife and two kids. I enjoy reading and writing books.